About the Author

Dudley Stewart was born in Manchester and raised in Sussex. After struggles in school and receiving a late diagnosis of autism in 2017, he began to focus his mind and vivid imagination into writing.

Hope you enjoy

Dudley Stewart

Diary of a Distant Star

Dudley Stewart

Diary of a Distant Star

Olympia Publishers
London

www.olympiapublishers.com
OLYMPIA PAPERBACK EDITION

A CIP catalogue record for this title is
available from the British Library.

ISBN: 978-1-80074-357-1

This is a work of fiction.
Names, characters, places and incidents originate from the writer's
imagination. Any resemblance to actual persons, living or dead, is
purely coincidental.

First Published in 2022

Olympia Publishers
Tallis House
2 Tallis Street
London
EC4Y 0AB

Printed in Great Britain

Dedication

I dedicate this book to my family.

Acknowledgements

Thank you to my mum, Alison, to my dad, Gordon, and elder brother, James, for encouraging me and helping me through dark times.

Day 0

After a very disastrous crash landing, in which I felt my entire skeleton shake violently, I had a few short seconds of unconsciousness.

When I awoke I found that luckily I survived, somehow I came away from the crash with only minor cuts, bruises and scratches and a dislocated arm.

Thankfully after checking the ships status, it seems there are no structural damage, no hull breaches and the ships window shutters are still closed after closing them during the emergency in case of broken glass and air breaches (as protocol states).

Then knowing the extent of my injuries, I first looked for the ships doctor the ever-pompous Dr Kevin Monroe, it didn't take long to find the doc dead. His demise unexpectedly sadden me as I never liked him, so I can only assume I must have some sort of head injury. His death must have been instantaneous, because of the awkward angle of his head from the body, I can only conclude it must have been a broken neck, but I'm no doctor.

My next action was to seek out the other crew members, but I am sad to say all other crew members are deceased, including my good friends Gary Bennett and Damian Smith.

Pushing my grief aside for now, my next action

was to sort out my dislocated arm, so going back to the medical bay I check the ships data to find out how to reposition my arm.

After an hour of searching page after page of the medical information, (most of which I found confusing and sickening), I found the data I needed. I then picked up some morphine pills, (just enough to dull the coming pain), then grabbed a sturdy medical bandage, tethered it to a medical locker use for storing medical supplies and wrapped it around my arm securely then held it tightly in my hand, (hopefully this will work first time, I don't want to do this again). Slipping a pill under my tongue and letting it dissolve, the taste was awful, gritty and seem to linger. When the effects of the meds took hold I counted to three and pulled my body away snapping the shoulder into place, and I must confess even with the small dose of morphine, the pain shot though my arm, though my chest and into every vein throughout my body, the pain made my eyes water so much so I couldn't see.

Just then I started to pass out letting go of the tether and collapsing to the floor and my last thoughts just before I lost consciousness was, I should of have had more morphine but at least it bloody well worked.

Day 1

I awoke startled with fright, a nightmare of my drugged addled mind.

As I sat up, with the pain throbbing though my arm, I looked around the room hoping briefly that the crash, my dead friends and horrors of being alone on the ship, was nothing more than only part of my darkest nightmare.

Now remembering the state of the situation I decided to take care of the deceased, first I moved, (with immense pain shooting throughout my damaged arm, accumulating into my shoulder), the bodies one by one by holding under the arms and dragging very slowly.

When all twelve bodies were in the quarters of Dr Monroe and placed with hands by their sides, when they all looked dignified, I said a few words and weep silently over my deceased crew members including the doc unexpectedly.

Then I walked out of the room, locked the door and lowered the temperature of the now newly made morgue to preserve them until help arrived and they can be returned home to their families, but for now this is where they rest in their makeshift tomb.

Next with tears in my eyes I check the communications system, sadly going though the systems data it seems that the subspace communications are severely damage and only the sub-light radio beacon system is working and even when the first transmission is sent it would take approximately a year to get to Earth.

So with no other options I have activated the system set the ships clock to UK time, (my country of origin), and checked the food and water supplies.

After checking the supplies, I had a very small lunch but contrary to what it says on the clock system, (which displayed 12:44pm), it didn't feel quite right, I check the other time zones but all of them felt wrong, I deduced that this planet must have a different orbit and day cycle, though I need more concrete evidence to prove such a deduction other than my gut instinct.

At this point my mind turned to my supplies, my water will last as long as I need it as long as the water recycling system functions with no glitches, food on the other hand would only last, even with great rationing, three to four months at the most.

My only option is to venture out onto this planet and see if I can gather more food supplies, luckily I have basic school days science, so I can check for most poisons but even then there will be great risk.

But for now before I can go outside I must modify the ships outer self-scan system to check for a breathable atmosphere.

Day 2

I had what must have been about an hours sleep after dozing off at the ships control system, I awoke with a shock as the alarm sounded for 8am, still very tired I realised I had worked though the night, which seemed much longer than normal.

The most frustrating part was after working non-stop I couldn't reprogram and modify the ships OSS (outer scan system).

When going to use the facilities on an occasion I heard some strange noises, which sounded as if something was outside scratching at the ship's hull to get in. Am I going mad I pondered to myself? I then started to hope that if it does gets in and does kill me please don't let me die on the toilet, I thought of the news on earth of such situation and got chills to think that history may remember me as the guy that survived a crash landing on an unknown planet but got killed by something while sitting on the toilet.

Pushing that thought aside, I will continue to try to modify the ships system and try to forget the possibility of something getting in. But I must confess all of this anxiety is causing me constant stomach pains.

I did think I got over this anxiety and pains, but then again I've never been stranded with the grim reaper looming beside me, waiting.

Day 3

After yet another sleepless night, I still could not modify the OSS. I got so frustrated I nearly grabbed the nearest tool and started whacking the blasted machine, thankfully I was able to calm myself.

So from 10am I slept a few hours. I awoke at 1:39pm, the sleep refreshed my mind and after I had a very quick shower to ration water, I check the system one more time, and came to the conclusion that it was above my intellect to sort out the system and decided to stop trying.

Still knowing my predicament, I came up with a plan; I was going to step outside the ship in an emergency space suit. The problem is that the suit is designed for quick outside repairs on the ship's hull and only has enough air to last no more than thirty minutes, but hopefully there is an atmosphere that can sustain life.

If there is breathable air I can remove the suit and start my new temporary life on an uninhabited planet, if there is no air then I must return to the safety of the ship and try and come up with a new plan.

After I checked the ships space suit, I used some duct tape to attach a portable device able to scan the local environment and give a quick analyst, but it takes about thirty minutes to get a full scan so it will be cutting it close. While sorting out the suit I again heard the scratching like sound, there must be something out there

I thought to myself, but another part of me thought I was going crazy from being alone.

So knowing what could happen I had a semi-large meal using supplies set aside for the last days, not eaten because of working of the OSS and set my alarm for 10am tomorrow.

Day 4

Today is the day, 10am, well technically 10:10am; I put on my suit, went to the air lock and close the door to the inner ship, then open the door to my fate.

Once outside I was beside myself with wonder, the sight I saw. Vast blue skies, the green leaves of the trees and grass, plus the definite signs of life, (by signs of life, I mean of the unidentified animal excretion I had just stepped in).

Due to the similarity to earth, I felt optimistic for the first time since the crash.

I then activated the device strapped to my arm, and waited, while passing the time I check the ship in great detail, other than the obvious dents from the crash, the ship seems in an ok condition, except for the apparent signs of scratches from a creature, and from the height of the mark about the size of an average house cat. This must have been the cause of the noises I been hearing over the last two days, and thought, no I hoped, please let it be cute and fluffy.

Then only fifteen minutes outside, a clumsy fool that I am, got my suit snagged on a tree branch while exploring nearby tearing the fabric slightly, knowing the air breach in the suit I quickly held my breath and ran to the ship.

When I got there I tried to open the door, but in my

panic I couldn't. So, knowing I will most likely perish. I thought sod it and took a deep breath, to my surprise I didn't die, so then I removed my helmet and breathed in the air and I was totally fine, no breathlessness, no apparent poisons and no death. The air was like being on Earth, but fresher. It was then I asked myself; how friendly is it and where were the life forms that lived here?

This will have to wait; my first objective is to find an edible food supply.

So I decided that I would check the local area, and what I found is astonishing and at the same time a problem. The flora of this planet is somewhat different than Earth's. It has flowers and leaves most of which are not on Earth and most likely have never been seen before anywhere man has been.

But while looking for something I may know is edible a thought ran though my mind, what if this planet has different weather patterns, like acid rain?

It most likely hasn't as most plant life known to man cannot survive in such an extreme weather phenomena like that, but still uncertainty looms. As I looked at a rather unique looking flower, which was like a dandelion but with pink petals and leaves that looked thin and serpent like, I noticed an insect the size of a hand. The creature was a type of beetle by the look of its large dome-like shell but has six large legs like a daddy long-legs spider. Each leg was the length of an average hand and the creature was latched onto a large tree, the markings on its back were black strips on a field of shinning green, when I went closer to get more detail the bug flew away on wings of translucent green, the size of an average index finger, the hum of the wings fluttering though the air was like the sound of a giant wasp, angry and ready to attack. As I watched it fly away, the sound diminishing into the wilderness and I truly realised that I was somewhere extraordinary.

When the sky began to darken, I walked back to the ship and looked around the night sky and wondered what other creatures are out there.

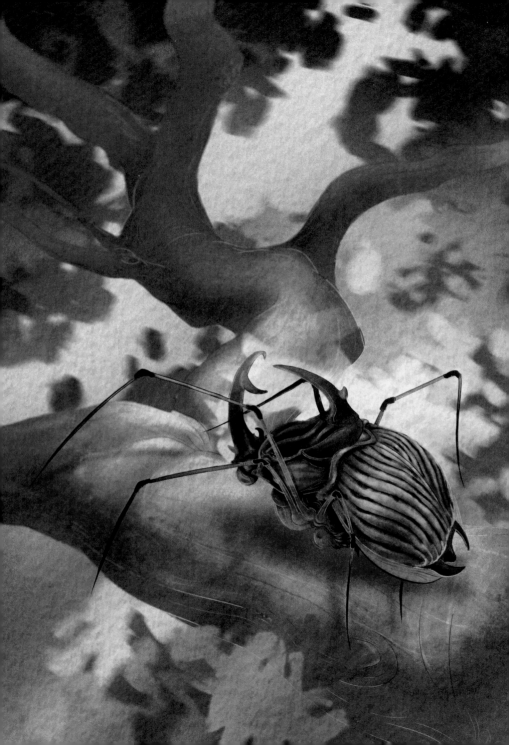

Day 5

This morning I began to try some knife throwing for hunting and defence; the only room big enough for such practice is the tech bay, where the controls of most of the ships energy and computer reside. As I threw the first knife, I accidentally hit the OSS panel. As the handle of the blade made contact with the control screen it awoke and upon checking the data read out, the blasted thing seem to be modified and working as I wanted it to days ago, when it started to hum to begin its work the only thought that went through my mind was, you bastard, if only I hit it when I wanted to.

So I grabbed a wrench and whacked it in anger and the machine shut down with whiny squeal, typical.

So stepping out again onto this new and strange world armed with three large knifes, freshly sharpened, obtain though the kitchen and a freshly charged standard issue stun gun from the armoury, I went in search of food.

In my search I saw many types of bird like creatures flying through the air but I didn't get a close look at any of them to make a note. Then while searching around some bushes for something edible, I discovered a strange creature, it made a weird growling sound while it ate, the growl itself is not to similar to the average housedog, the look however is anything but, for that reason I called it a Growler.

Its two thick legs hold up a tiny mass, which is in the shape of an egg with the tip of the egg pointing to the east, south-east via the side view with its rear ending like that of a semi-deflated balloon tail, and small lanky arms it uses to pick up prey to its wide pink mouth full of sharp jagged fangs. I couldn't see what it was eating as what it was holding was so mangled and chewed, it was unrecognisable, when it was done it looked around itself with its large bulbous eyes which shone in the light as a tainted yellowed green. Its skin colour similar to my pale peach was covered on the top of its head going down to its back was a brownish red coloured hair. I theorize it must protect it from the sunlight.

When it started to walk away I decided to follow, to see if it could lead me to some kind of food source, what it did lead me to was a clear water pond, great, if my water supply dries up, but I must first test it for parasites or other deadly bacteria, I also learnt more about the growler, it has a straw like tongue that unravels from it wide gapping mouth that is forked like a snakes and is hollow, it slurps the water like my toothless uncle slurps his tomato soup, noisily and disgustingly.

Then after it was quenched it decided to have a crap, right there in front of me and I'll tell you now, not only did it put me off malt loaf the stink made my eyes water, so I got away as fast as I could.

As I got close to the ship the clouds started to darken, and as I still had no idea of the rain on this planet, I got inside very quickly. The rain then started to fall about fifteen minutes later, it seemed like a huge storm, going by the thunder, lighting and the wind blasting the hull with great force.

Knowing the storm may not pass for a while I decided to grab my e-reader and read for the rest of the day, and had an early night.

Day 6

I was woken in the middle of the night by a large crash, unluckily for me the ship was filling with smoke very fast, I worked my way through the smoke to find that the ship was on fire, due to the storm still raging outside I can only surmise that lighting must have struck the ship, my only thought was to escape.

With smoke stinging my eyes, my vision obstructed and sweat running down my face, I felt my way along the ship quickly finding my way back to my quarters, I grabbed my diary recorder and my sketchbook and ran for the airlock.

At this time, my breathing is getting very hard as the heat of the confined air started to burn my lungs, but with strength of will I pushed on.

Knowing the layout of the ship helped and eventually I got to the air lock and opened it with a rush, the door felt heavy when I tried to rotate the hatch lock, my fingers kept slipping and fumbling on the lock, and I started to panic it also didn't help with the sweat on my palms. After quickly getting myself together I was able to open the lock, at this time breathing was near impossible, my lungs hurt so much I collapsed to the floor on all fours and crawled through the door, and pushed the door closed and as I did the smell of burning flesh invaded my nostrils.

With the door shut I went to open the outer door

but as I put my hands on the heavy handle, a small bang sounded from beyond the door I had just closed and though the porthole of the door a rush of flames hurried past, at this moment I felt my heart pound in my chest as fear took hold of me and the heat started to rise more and more.

Finally getting the outer door open, I burst though it and ran for the openness of the outside world, as I looked back upon the ship I saw what I escaped, flames raged through the entire ship, destroying all within and nearly incinerated me with it.

Then realising about the power supply, and the small explosion I heard before, it came to me to run, and run I did.

After about two minutes of running a huge explosion bellowed though the air, the shockwave felled the trees nearby as it radiated outwards from the ship, (or what was left of the ship), as the sound echoed through the air, I fell to the ground covered my head with my hands just in case of small projectiles of debris.

When I felt I was safe I unclasped my hands and turned to lay down on my back and looked at the fading night sky. I was left speechless of the beauty of the many bright stars; unlike anything you would see on earth due to light pollution.

While observing the sky and though the fluttering wings of scared birds, I notice this planet has two moons, one slightly smaller but just as bright, the beauty of which astounded me.

As the darkness started to wash away by the coming light of the sun and I watched with wonder, then I stumbled to the nearest tree and fell slowly asleep.

My sleep did not last long as suddenly from out of nowhere I felt something drop on my lap, as my eyes open I was staring into the widest eyes of some sort of animal.

When I moved the creature jumped of my lap and sat waiting on the floor in front of me like a dog.

The cute wide eyes blinked and then continued to stare, hoping it was friendly I held out my hand, looking back now maybe that was a silly thing to do as it could have had some sort of disease like rabies or even was poisonous, but thankfully this was not the case, the creature pushed its head to my hand like a cat wanting to be petted.

I decided to call my new discovery a Tree cat, for its cat-like head and paws and black fur with lime green stripes circling its Lemur like body like rings, its tail was long and fluffy, a cross between a cats and a lemur.

As I started to walk away it in turn started to follow me, as I turn it turn, as I stopped it stopped, I the decided to try and pick it up and amazingly it seem very docile with me as if it was tamed, and even pushed its head into my free hand again to be petted and I thought could this be the creature that scratched up the ship's hull.

I went back to the ship to see the extent of the damage and my heart sank as all what was left was a smoking heap of metal and I wondered to myself how could this happen, as the ship has metal plating that should have repelled the lighting strikes.

After mulling over it for a while and coming up with nothing, I thought of the fact that I needed new shelter and more than ever a food source.

So setting off into the unknown of this planet and with a new companion by my side, I went in search of the food and shelter I needed while not going very far from the water pond I found a few days ago.

I first started to look for food, after about what felt like an hour of walking I began to get hungry, when it struck and my stomach started to growl with fury the Tree cat pick up its head and look around like a Meerkat, as if thinking "what was that".

As the growls got louder, and more frequent the Tree cat look around; it was like the animal was looking out for a predator.

After approximately another hour or so I decided to rest, but knowing there could be something that could kill me, I thought it would be safer to climb a tree to rest and get away from the ground, big mistake.

After my version of climbing, which includes broken

branches, falling, cuts and bruises, I got a third of the way up about a two metre from the ground.

Getting settled and balanced, I relaxed for about ten minutes, when a red like spider drop down on my leg and started to crawl along my body, as I was startled with fright and trying to brush the thing off I fell out of the tree luckily on some bushes, but still it hurt like hell, then jolted up as I felt more things crawl over me. I discovered some sort of green ant like insect, brushing them off quickly with fear bursting though my veins while the Tree cat watched with interest.

After feeling I got them all off I started to worry, what if anything bit me, there could be poisons or viruses going through my veins and who knows what they could do, so I stripped down to my underwear and check for bites for what I could see there was none, but I couldn't check my back, so still worrying I thought, sod it I would take my chances and put on my clothing again to continue my search and if I die at least I could say I died from unknown creatures on an unknown planet.

When it started to get dark on yet another unproductive day I decided to make camp near the water pond where I saw the Growler, as darkness settles I tried to make fire, using sticks from nearby my camp, and even though I was taught how to make campfires by my granddad when I was six, camping in the local woods near his house, I couldn't start the blasted thing and when I did the fire went out, but still I kept trying.

After getting a spark I finally got the fire started, it felt like hours passed, I stayed very close to the light and I grabbed a thick broken tree branch to use as a weapon and all I thought was shame I didn't grab one of the knifes when the ship went up in smoke, and how stupid was I to grab only my sketch book, what good would that be in any kind of trouble.

Just as I was about to fall asleep I notice the Tree cat was gone, I looked around the camp and suddenly felt very worried for the thing, but I knew I couldn't look for it in the darken forest nearby, I just hoped at that time that it would be ok, and still with worry in mind, I laid down and fell asleep with the sound of what I assume are nocturnal bird calls and howls of various kinds out in the distance to keep me company.

Day 7

That night while I slept, I dreamt of the most awful things happening to the Tree cat, I never knew that my imagination could make up such things. I awoke with a start in the bright daylight, relieved that my nightmare was over.

By my side was the Tree cat, curled up to me with its head on my lap, and all I felt was joy, that it wasn't hurt in anyway. It was then I noticed a weird creature near my feet it was some sort of, what I can only assume is a kind of dead Rat. It looked like a Rat on earth but on closer inspection its ears were pointy like an elf and had in its mouth the teeth like a Dogs but tiny, and it came to me that it must have been caught and delivered by the Tree cat.

It was then I decided to try and keep this helpful little Tree cat creature, I tore a portion of one of my shirts sleeve and carefully wrapped it around my new friends neck like a collar and decided to name him Ringo after its markings and not the member of the band that I heard of once in history class.

I decided to eat the Rat as I was so hungry and eating anything on this planet is a risk, I started to skin it with a sharp small branch I adapted and removed offal from its body and threw them to one side, as I did so Ringo devoured them quickly while I put the rat over the fire to cook it.

While I did so, Ringo watched with a confused look, as if wondering why I am doing this.

When I was satisfied the meat was fully cooked I ate it like a starved Dog in a butchers, the little meat there was itself was tough like a boot, but tasty like Lamb, when I was done I thanked Ringo and scratched him behind the ear which he seems to love.

We went to the water source and decided to drink the water, even though I could not test it like I wanted to. It also put me at ease when Ringo started to drink it. So using my hands as a cup I quenched my thirst, the water tasted very fresh, better than anything you get out of taps on earth and certainly a lot better than the recycled water on the ship.

As the day went on the planet got hotter and hotter, and sweat began to cover my entire body. The only thing I could do was removed my jacket even then it seemed to do nothing. I then decided I needed to find or make some sort of container to carry water, especially if the heat on this planet can get like this every day. On my search I wondered if this planet is in it summer season and started to worry what if it wasn't would it get even hotter? I truly hoped this is as hot as it could get and it would go back to the nice cool sunny days just like they were when I first stepped out onto this world.

When it seemed that the sun was overhead and burning into my flesh I scurried over to the nearest tree with Ringo following me. After what felt like an hour I started to get hungry, but moving in this heat was crazy hard, every movement felt exhausting and impossible, it was then I looked at Ringo and wondered, "how the hell does he feel and cope with his fur?" I then realised there is nobody around, so I could remove my clothing and cool down.

When I removed my clothing to the point in which I was only in my underwear. Ringo looked at me wondering what I was doing, I sat back down in the shade of the tree and still if felt like I was boiling like an egg in water. Every so often I moved to get water from the pond and still the thought went through my mind of a container, I started to hope if I could make one out of a hollowed-out bit of wood, it that's when I broke off a thick piece of wood from the tree that I hid under from the sun and began carving it into shape, realising how the bloody difficult it would be as I had no tools.

Then I held the wood tightly and started to whack it with rage on the ground, shouting in anger with sweat streaming over my naked flesh and the local birds flying away from the nearby trees, and Ringo creeping away with fear.

Still with anger clouding my mind I threw the chunk of wood with all of my might. It was at this point I saw Ringo, his wide eyes looked at me with fear, and then my anger was substituted with guilt. I felt so much guilt for scaring not only the birds from the trees in which I wanted to study. But I scared my only friend that helped me when I needed it, I held out my arms and I said softy "I'm so sorry" hoping he would come to me and forgive me, he did the opposite and ran, it was then I was left alone.

When it began to get dark the heat cooled down,

and I started to worry if Ringo was all right, I called out for him in the darkness with only an Owl-like response. I then decided to walk out to find him; it came to me to light a fire as then I could find my way back in the night. It took what seemed like forever to start the blasted thing and when I did it felt like the night was getting old and the moons where big and high in the sky like eyes watching over me, I needed sleep and the tiredness started to take hold quickly dampening my senses and hunger weakening my strength, it was then I made up my mind. Ringo was scared of me now and he knew this forest better than me, but I must at least try after all he was my friend, I got up with a stagger and walked with a wobble to the nearest tree for balance, but as I walked a couple of steps I fell and couldn't move from hunger and tiredness. I then slowly fell asleep.

Day 8

I awoke with a start worrying for my new friend Ringo, it was then I saw cuddled up to my leg asleep was Ringo and at my feet another Rat, the happiness I felt was extreme. I gave Ringo a good deal of pampering for his help and as an apology for my temper.

When he looked up with his wide eyes I said, "thank you" and "sorry for my actions".

I prepared the Rat like I did before but this time I gave Ringo some of the cooked meat, he first smelt it and then tried it then he ate it with delight.

When I was done I thought heat or not I needed to search for food. It was then I saw flying over my camp a type of bird, it landed in a tree nearby and when I looked at it from where I was sitting I notice it was like a cross between a Pterodon and a normal bird, it had wings like a Pterodon with small feathers on its wings, it held itself like a Bat using its claws on its wings for grip and balance then looking around on its two legs. Its beak was like a hawks with a sharp point, for what I could see it seems to have a crack like mark on the beak but I couldn't be sure. It had two long tails about a foot long like a Rat with a bundle of feathers on the end of the two long trails of flesh. Its feathers shone in the light of the sun and were dark blue, nearly black with a few red patches on its wings and on its tails. The head had largish feathers like a crown maybe used to attract mates, the overall size by eye and excluding the tails of the creature was approximately just under a metre, but I again could be wrong. It reminded me of the creatures on earth that linked dinosaurs to birds.

I put on my trousers and shirt and wrapped my jacket around my waist, and started on my new quest to find more food. While going through the forest I found a sharp stone and I left markings on the trees to find my way back to the pond, but hopefully I won't need to if find more water along the way.

So with Ringo on my shoulders like some sort of scarf. I found a small clearing and as I walked into it Ringo started to get restless, he began to bury his head into my neck to hide like he knew he shouldn't be here, but with curiosity filling my mind I stepped slowly into the clearing. As I did so, about six or seven more Tree cats jumped down around me, strange thing was that the others compared to Ringo were twice the size. As I stumble round to see them all as they all had various stripes, marking and colour combos, when I walked close to one it started to hiss at me and one, with brown fur and green stripes like a Zebra on earth, tried to bite me and all I thought was, "you evil little git".

I looked at Ringo to see if he could be some sort of help, but as I looked into his eyes all I saw was fear, at this point I had no idea why but I would soon know. I put my hands up as they all crowded around me circling me like some sort of pack of Hyenas waiting tear their prey to shreds. It was then I realised it wasn't me they were after. They were after Ringo, for when I was pushed up against the nearby tree on the outskirts of the clearing the tried to get him. I covered Ringo with my arms and ran for the forest as they pursued us. After a while of running the group of Tree cats broke away and stopped the attack, the problem was now we were lost in the expanse of trees, the only good thing was the shade from the sun, but even then it was still stifling. As we recovered from the run, with me trying to get my breath back, Ringo began to calm down. I wondered why the other tree cats attacked, the only thing I could come up with was the fact that Ringo was smaller than the others, and maybe he was some kind of runt of the litter and the species, instinctively try to "remove" the weak link of the group and Ringo escaped. I would like to study the group but not at the expense of Ringo's safety.

So with no other possible action I put Ringo on my shoulder and petted him, and walked on into the unknown wilderness.

The weather was getting hot and the air felt warm to breath, and the only respite was the occasional howl of cooling wind through the trees. After a while of trekking onwards we escaped the trees, and came upon a field, there seemed to be a rabbit burrow, so hoping for food, I grabbed my jacket that I wrapped around my waist and waited, as it started to get late in the day I notice a small nose coming up though one of the burrows, I slowly stepped towards the hole and as the rabbit poked its ears out of the holes I pounced. The rabbit jumped out of the hole and into my jacket, as I struggle with it, it kicked out and struck me in the family jewels making me lose my grip and it jumped towards the burrow and looked back, and I swear with pain shooting though my body, I'm sure it had a glint in its eye like it was saying, "ha can't get me", it took some time for me to recover when it did I check to see if all was ok down there and waited for the rabbit to come back out of the hole.

When darkness fell, it did decide to take another chance this time I was successful in my task and was able to wrap it in my jacket and was able to hold it between my legs while holding its feet with one of my hands and its head with the other. Now I had the hard task to kill it.

I held the Rabbit and still with its body in my legs, I snapped its neck, and like that he was dead, at this moment I started to weep uncontrollably and constantly kept saying sorry to the dead animal. When I pulled myself together I unwrapped my jacket and I said thank you to the creature which I am sure was a Rabbit like on earth, the only difference was this Rabbit had large tufts of fur on the tips of its ears, so using the sharp stone I found earlier I gutted the Rabbit and again left the offal to Ringo, which he devoured very quickly, I cooked the meat and ate it like a zombie in a fat club. I took the bones and made a fork and knife by sharpening them with the sharp stone, and I took the skin and thought I could use it some time, not one part of the creature was going to be wasted.

After what felt like a hearty meal, I heard the sound of water dripping from somewhere, I looked round and found a small blocked up river nearby, I assume this is what the Rabbit drinks when it comes out of the burrow. When I unblocked it a small stream of water like a tap came towards me and using my hands I drank the fresh water with Ringo drinking beside me. When I was done I went back to the camp fire and I laid down and looked up at the night sky and wondered if help would come, but when I felt Ringo cuddle up next to me, I felt different, like I wanted to stay and study this world and its inhabitants. This constant conflict of desires plagued me that night and the only way I was able to forget it, was to look at the bright and wondrous night sky with its two moons and billions stars. As I looked around the sky I noticed a Moth like bug fluttering around the fire and over time more turned up some of them died trying to fly into the flames. I heard the Owl like sounds from the other night in the distance again, and I wondered after thinking about the Rabbit I ate, what other creatures are on this planet and would be like animals on earth. While thinking on this subject for some time I fell asleep, with the noise of the night in the distance.

Day 9

Kill me I thought, as my stomach was causing me to have the potty trots, my God it was bad. The more I moved the more I went, it must be because of the new water supply on this planet, my body must just have to get used to it.

Over the course of about three hours I had the runs, but thank God my body started to recover. When it did I started to hunt for yet another meal.

During my search I discovered more unusual plant life, one of which was a red daisy-like plant the size of a earth rose with no leaves on the stem at all, I looked  at the whole plant bed but there was nothing, I decided to look at the roots of the plant, so I dug my way into the ground and removed one of the plants to get a better look, and I must say the roots are like nothing I've never seen before, it had strange hard carapace cylinders covering the root strands, it looked like a cardboard robot costume with card tubes covering the top and lower arms leaving the elbow uncovered to move, this is how the root looked.

I wondered why the plant would evolve like this; it was then I noticed movement in the soil near where I dug, and waited very still like a rock and hoped to see what was living in the dirt. But all I saw was a little nose like a moles poking out, maybe to smell the air, after my near encounter I theorized that this unknown creature must eat the roots of plants, and in turn the plants evolved to try and protect itself with a hard shell around its most needed body part.

When I continued my search I came across a tree with moss on it, but mixed growing within the moss was a strange yellow flower, it had four distinct petals with tiny tooth like grooves on the tip of each of the petals.

The flowers were growing from the moss and sprouting out and towards the sky as if it was trying to reach it, plus the moss had a Caterpillar-like bug crawling over it, maybe to eat the moss or the flowers, within it, the Caterpillar was hairy like on earth but was thin like a worm and had skin of bright yellow with brown blotches over both ends and over the body was brown stripes.

After all these amazing discoveries I couldn't help but wonder is there anymore.

After what felt like hours of walking and still looking for food, I started to wonder if I should have tried to catch the Mole from earlier to eat. Around my neck Ringo was snoozing, then suddenly his head looked up like a Meerkat, then buried it deeply into my neck tightly, it was then I saw a small Ferret creature it had huge ears like a mini fluffy Elephant and light brown fur.

As it scurried into a bush I followed it to try and catch it for food. In a tiny clearing behind the bush and surrounded by tall grass the Ferret sat, as I got closer the animal saw me and hissed like a Cat. This did not dissuade me to try and catch it, but as it ran for the apparent safety of some thick overgrown grass, the grass suddenly wrapped around it like a Snake holding it tightly then

 in the dirt a large round fang filled mouth opened up and started to chew the Ferret slowly starting with its fluffy tail, then legs and so on, the gory sight made me sick to my stomach. As the fangs shredded the flesh of the poor Ferret, the sight of blood put me off any food for a good while, I tried to help the Ferret but it was dead before my legs would move from the shock, as the thing was still eating the body,

I turn and ran to get away from the thing dodging the long grass patches just in case of more attacks, and I started to think that Ringo knew about the crazy monster I called the Bite-weed.

After running back to my camp from the night before, I tried to forget the incident but the cries of the Ferret was deep in my mind, it was at this point my childhood copping mechanism came back, when something scared me deeply I would fall asleep, I got a drink of water to keep myself awake but it was no good. I sat down in my camp and quickly fell asleep with the glow of twilight covering me. My last memory of the day was seeing Ringo run away again, wondering why and scared for its safety the worry made my eyes even more tired it was then I fell asleep.

That night I had horrid nightmares about Ringo being eaten by the monstrous Bite-weed, over and over again I had them, I awoke during the night covered in sweat and I looked for Ringo around me but saw nothing, I fell back to sleep and the nightmares started again getting more bloody as the night when on.

Day 10

I awoke early and still there was no sign of Ringo, I called for him and felt a fool as the though struck me that, "he doesn't even know the name I gave him".

I sat back down by the burnt-out fire, as the smoke bellowed up into the blue sky I thought I should look for Ringo, after all he has a blue rag around his neck. Then I looked over the field with all the trees around it and dotted throughout the land, my heart sank as thinking where he might be in this vast expanse. Knowing it would take days maybe months to look everywhere for him, I decided the best thing is to wait around the camp hoping he would return and I gave myself a time limit of a day to wait, after a day and still nothing I must conclude the worst.

It was then the potty trots came back because of the worry. I went behind a bush and looked around thoroughly for Bite-weeds and did my business. When I got back Ringo was sitting next to the camp looking around, and when he saw me, he ran to my leg and brushed up against me like a cat would to a plant it scent on you. I pick it up holding him like a baby and tickle it belly and pampered him while at the same time telling him off, (like he notices).

Knowing I must begin my search for food and shelter, I pushed my fears aside and continued on with

Ringo safely around shoulders.

On my search I found a strange plant that was in the opposite direction that I had walked yesterday. There were five of them plus they were all equally distance apart from each other and had all the same number of petals and leaves, the leaves looked like average leaves seen on lavender and all the plants had three each all very similar sizes. The flowers themselves had tiny heads covering a stalk about the size of a foot, (give or take a few centimetres), and each head look like a bell made of bright pink petals. In each one it had three yellow stamens. I again decided to dig one up to look at the root system, little did I know they were all connected, the roots looked very strange, it was like a greenish-white table with the plants sprouting from it and the roots underneath it digging into the ground.

When I covered the plants with dirt again, a Bee-like bug buzzed pass my ear, as it did so Ringo looked around himself and twitched his ears, maybe to hear better but he was wasting his time for the Bee flew straight to the pink-bells, (which I had named them), and did what Bees do on earth. Being very careful to get a better

look, as I don't know if it has poison when it stings, (even though I'm not allergic to bee stings, but this Bee could be different). The bee had two portions of its body covered in fuzz and six legs, like bees on earth, it had large wings, which would account for the louder buzzing and had what looked like two lower mandibles and hooks on its two chins, the colour was still yellow and black but instead of stripes it had spots, after noting this new find I continued my search.

About a few hours of just normal green bushes, large trees and blank patches of ground, I found a cave surrounded and hidden by trees. The cave was large and seemed to go deep into the planets depths. I was happy that I found such a place but was apprehensive about the inside and what could be lurking deep with its dark chambers, as the last thing I need now, is to find something worse than the Bite-weeds.

I decided that while it was still light outside, I was going to search the cave a little way in, just to see if anything could be living in there that I may not want to coexist with.

So I made a makeshift torch, using more of my shirt and a branch from a nearby tree, it took ages to make as I had to first make a campfire I thrust the torch into it blazing centre to light the bloody thing, after it was done and my torch was lit, I set off into the darkness.

I was scared like hell near to the point of the trots coming back, but what put me at ease was seeing Ringo not moving for he always seemed to know if something bad was nearby, like the Bite-weed incident yesterday.

I was only meant to go a few feet into the cave, but I heard what sounded like running water deep inside so I decided to trek on.

With only a small light to guide me I soon came to a large opening, it looked like and underground beach with stalagmites and stalactites scattered around the floor and ceiling, I went to the edge of the body of water and using my hands tasted a small amount of it, thankfully the water was drinkable, in fact it tasted filtered like some sources of water on earth. I decided then and there to

make this cave my home for the immediate future. So going back to the mouth of the cave. Where I had made my fire, I started to make preparations to defend myself and my new home. I grabbed more branches of nearby trees, and using rocks from the cave I slowly make wooden spikes and placed them around the cave mouth, like the old fashion wooden defences, I'd learned about from history class in school, making sure there was room for me to escape. But if anything bigger than me came, it would give me at least a chance to defend myself, when night fell I tried to dig two additional holes into the soft ground just outside the five stakes I made during the day, like a moat for extra defence, but with not eating again I felt very tired and took my chances and fell asleep. As I did so Ringo, who was sitting beside me as I made my defences, ran off again into the dark wilderness.

I would have followed because of what happen yesterday, but with him being quite fast and me being exhausted from hunger, I just couldn't and fell asleep with worry yet again on my mind.

Day 11

When I awoke I found Ringo sound asleep next to me with two more Rats at my feet.

I prepared them like I've done before, and eating most of the meat as I gave some to Ringo which he seemed to enjoy. After eating I started work on the last two stakes, the process to about two hours or so.

After I was done making and placing the wooden spikes I went in search of more food, it didn't take long to find a Rat within the trees around the cave. I crept up to it and using my jacket, pounced and caught it. I broke the neck of the Rat and took it back to my cave, putting the dried Rabbit skin I kept from days ago out like a tiny blanket, I placed the Rat on it and took of my shirt and used it to cover up my spoils, then I went out hunting again.

I had just found another Rat, and was about to try the same thing again. I was just about to pounce when shrieking noises came from beyond the tree about a couple of metres behind my cave, and my prey ran of scared. Angry but curious, I strolled over to the noise, trying to keep silent as I did so.

I got near to the tree line and crouched down trying to keep hidden. In the clearing beyond where I was standing, I saw multiple Growlers in what seemed to be some kind of mating season display.

There were some growlers like the one I saw previously, they were scattered around, but others, which I gather, were male due to shrieking noises they made and the longer hair of various colours that adorned them like lion manes, around their heads. The males were doing some kind of dance, hoping on one leg then the other while turning around in one place, the display was fascinating to watch, the males danced while the females strolled around like if they were window shopping, trying to decide the best mate. Just then a Rat like the one I was trying to catch scurried into the clearing and all the males looked at it then gave chase, then showing off their speed one of the males caught it and stepped on it, then while the Rat was stunned it crouched down and grabbed it with its arms and bit off the poor thing's head. Then instead of eating the Rat the male took it back to where it had been dancing and placed it in front of himself and started to dance again it was like the Rat was adornment, maybe to show he was the better hunter.

When a female chose her mate, she made a sound like Dog growling at an enemy, then she turn and waggled her bottom at the desired mate, maybe like a come-hither display. Then the male waddled over and started to scratch the female gentle over her body the female crouched and the male mounted. It was at this point I walked away to give them privacy after all I wouldn't want people watch me when I'm with my wife.

So continuing my search for food and with the cries of Growlers mating in the distance, I with, Ringo still asleep on my shoulders like he's been all day, walked on with hunger setting in again.

It was at this point I got angry of being constantly hungry and wondering that there must be more edible animals other than the Rats and the elusive Rabbits, then I began to consider the Growlers.

"After all," I thought "they maybe tasty, so grabbing a largish rock I walked back to the sound of the Growlers. On my way I saw a male Growler he seemed unique as he had only three toes instead of the usual four and blue hair which seemed normal for male Growlers but this one was different as was shorter and thin, he looked like he was alone, maybe this male couldn't find a mate, when he stopped to sniff the ground I readied the rock with the creature in my sights, I counted to three and nothing, I tried counted to three again and nothing, I just couldn't kill it for he seemed lonely, like me on this planet. I felt empathy for the creature, my mind finally free of hunger madness I looked at the rock and wondered, "Who the hell would this do, it's tiny".

After tiptoeing away from the lonely Growler, I started to walk back to camp in what felt like the afternoon sun. Back at my camp I looked at my food resources, the single rat. I looked at Ringo, (who was still fast asleep on my shoulders), and wondered if he could catch more rats for me, I picked him up and placed him on the floor, not even then did he awaken, I started worrying if he was dead, but my fear was push aside when I saw his little belly move from breathing. I waited out the rest of the day, I tended to the fire preparing for the evening; it was then I started to feel the loneliness of my situation, Ringo helps with that sometimes, but with no one to talk to I felt desolate, I was reminded of school, no friends, no one to talk to, and no one who seemed to care.

I started to sing just to try something to get the loneliness out of my mind, but it didn't really work. My childhood depression set in once more, like a black virus in my mind with its dark tendrils invading all the portions of my brain, and I was powerless to stop it.

It was then the lonely Growler walked up to camp through the wooden stakes, its bulbous eye shining in the light of the fire. In the twilight of the coming evening, I sat rigid wondering what to do. And I thought at that time, "those stakes are useless", I readied myself for a fight, but instead the Growler just waddled up to the fire and plonked itself down beside it, and folded its hands and sat calmly like a child in school, I didn't dare to go near it, just in case it attacked. I slowly moved up to Ringo preparing to keep him safe.

When night fell I tried not to sleep because of the stranger in camp, but in the long run it was no use, the tiredness took hold slowly but with force.

With my strength gone for the day I fell asleep without me even realising.

Day 12

I awoke with fright, realising that I had fallen asleep with a Growler in the camp.

I looked around, and noticed that the growler was gone and so was Ringo. I felt the fear and guilt take hold thinking the Growler had eaten Ringo, with that running through my mind, I could have saved Ringo by killing the Growler yesterday when I had the chance.

The thought of my friend's death was push aside with hope, when I notice there was no blood or other signs of attacks around camp. Then I started to worry if Ringo was chase into the wilderness. Then again I felt relief thinking that Ringo is a lot faster the Growler if yesterday's display was anything to go by. I remembered the mating ritual from yesterday and worry set in again, what if Ringo ran into the others.

Pushing that aside I went to get water from the back of the cave, when I returned I found Ringo sitting by the fire with yet another two Rats and a large rabbit, I looked at the Rabbit with wonder, did Ringo somehow drag this Rabbit? How when it was twice the size of himself, back to camp along with the two rats?

The other option was even stranger which was did the Growler from the night before bringing it for some reason, maybe like a thank you?

If the latter was the case, then the Growler must have

some sort of sentience to recognise the fact that I allowed it to stay near the fire and the emotion to feel gratitude. This was a very fascinating thought.

I then went to fillet the rat I caught yesterday, but the rat started to go putrid and decomposed in the heat, it was not fit for me to eat. So with lots more food I received from my friends, I began to worry it wouldn't last.

I then had a thought what about the cave, after all it was cooler in there than it was outside. So after gutting the creatures I took my new food supplies, and walked into the cave and it was a lot cooler, which I had never really noticed before, I hoped that the cave would somewhat cool the meat, like a meat locker but only time would tell.

So leaving the meat somewhere safe, I took one of the Rats and went back outside where I found Ringo sitting waiting for me, so preparing the food like always and sharing it with Ringo, I tucked into yet another tasty rat breakfast.

I realised then that I can't surviving on hand outs, I would make a weapon to catch my own prey like humans did when our species was young.

So with this thought running through my mind I broke a branch from a tree. I looked around and found a sharp rock in the cave, then using my shirt and tearing it up into strips. I made a makeshift spear with rags to spare, I tested it in the cave throwing against the cave wall, and it fell apart. I changed the design and tried again, it took a while for me to get it to work without breaking. Then I gathered more supplies and made and tested more spears, in the end I made three working weapons in which I sharpened for more effectiveness.

So I started to trek out once again into wilderness with Ringo by my side, (or on my shoulder), and a bloodlust for more food. Taking only one spear, I knew I could only make clear kill shots, I hoped my old school PE lessons in the javelin was somewhere still in my memory.

In what felt like the late afternoon I found a large animal. I called it the Lion-hog for the fact it looked like a wild Boar, but it had a tail like a lions, long and slender with the tuft of fur at the end, and it had four tusks and a matted mane like a Lions.

I observed it, waiting for my time to strike. When suddenly it seemed to screech in pain like a Pig in a blender and Ringo held onto me with its tiny claws, it was then I noticed the Hogs foot was being shredded by a Bite-weed. The lion-hog must have put its foot in it without realising.

The shrieking getting louder with each moment and Ringo's claws digging into me more and more with fear. I decided that I would put the Lion-hog out of its misery, for half of its leg was gone and it was bleeding out, so I jumped out and stab the Lion-hog with my spear in its head killing it instantly. Then I pulled the mangled leg as hard as I could and pulled it out of the Bite-weeds blender like mouth. Dodging the weed I dragged the Hog back slowly, but this took time. So with all my strength I pick it up and held it over my shoulders with Ringo atop the hog nipping at it all the way back. When I got back twilight was setting in and I put the dead creature next to the fire and using my spear I slowly cut of a leg of the beast and skinned it, then put it over the fire on a makeshift spit.

While it was cooking I open up the belly carefully and gutted the poor brute I of course threw the entrails to Ringo, which he ate, but couldn't finish so I threw the leftovers out of the camp.

Before that though, I put the rest of the hog into the cave with the other meat I collected, and I was surprised to find the cave colder than it was during the day, so I was happy that my cooling area may work.

I decided I needed a cup for washing water so I retrieved the Rabbit, that the Growler brought to me and removed it head and skinned it to the skull, I then took it outside and tipped the contents into the fire, it sizzled on impact, then rinsed the skull with water and held it over the fire to clean it and killing the germs.

When the leg was done cooking I removed it from the spit I didn't think would work, but amazingly it did. I then tucked in eating all I could when I was full I put my jacket on the floor nearby and put the leftovers on it for morning. I then removed the skull from the fire and went to the cave river and scooped up water in the skull and when back outside to boil it for cleaning, I did this so my water supply wasn't contaminated with blood and other harmful germs.

When the water had boiled I let it cool until I could use it without burning myself. I poured some onto one hand and then over the other and repeated. When I was satisfied I was clean I put the skull to one side, I realised I should have done that days ago, instead of just wiping my hand on my discarded shirt.

After all this was done I laid down to fall asleep. Before I drifted off I decided,

"Tomorrow I'm going to make a hammock, so I wouldn't have to sleep on the floor anymore."

Day 13

The next morning I tried to gather items to make my hammock, but was unsuccessful. All the materials I found were not long enough or strong enough. Even when weaved together, they didn't make my desired sleeping apparatus.

Annoyed by the set back, I went into my cave to my water supply had a drink using my hands, then I strolled over to my food, now ether I am losing my mind or my food has moved closer to the stream.

I moved it back to where I am sure I left it before, but this time left it behind a rock, so if it was moved I would definitely know. I checked my supplies before taking a rat for my breakfast all the meat was still there, so hopefully I'm just tired.

I went back to camp and grabbed one of my spears and went exploring this planet.

As I walk away from camp Ringo ran and crawled up my body and sat over my shoulders like always. After about two hours walk, I found yet many new plants but one stood out more, the plant was like a sunflower, but facing the opposite direction of the sun, and it seems as a result, it has dark purple petals, the leaves all had sharp points, like earths nettle bushes.

There was a number of them I removed one to see the roots and was astonished what came with it, while

the roots looked like normal sunflower roots, the creature that came with it wasn't really looking. It was like a small dragon with two tiny spikes on its back instead of wings, the tiny creatures teeth were blunt, most likely to chew roots of various plant life, it had small hands with two claws each that looked like two tiny shovels.

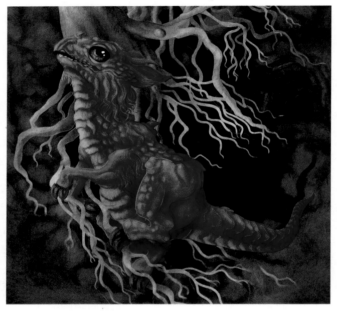

Its chunky legs melded with it small round body, and it's had shiny red scales covering its hide including its underbelly. Before I let it loose I crouched down to check the holes it dug, the holes looked like the typical tunnels made by underground animals, but had tiny shovel marks like some sort of escape tunnel made by a prisoner trying to get out of prison. After one last look at the creature I noticed it had deep black eyes and I wondered if it could see. I put my finger near its face and it only flinched when I got very close to its face. So I surmised it has bad eyesight but is not blind, I then click my fingers to check its hearing which was amazing as every click was noticed, so this made me wonder, why it didn't move when I removed the plant, as it must have heard me?

I let the Ground-dragon loose into its cave and walked on.

Yet another hour in to my exploration I found some mushrooms growing on a tree, the fungi looked like sky-blue tiny steps going a foot up the tree from the ground and each step had darker blue pigments, some even had slight yellow pigments around the edge.

I know next to nothing about fungi, I was not even going to try them or even touch them in case of ether poison or allergic reactions.

As I continued my walk I came across more plants, one was a flower but had green petals that looked like many leaves, the stalk had no leaves on it and its roots were very thick but other was normal.

The other plant was a blue rose with leaves nearly covering up the entire stalk. Each leaf has three large points at the tip and the roots had thin strands coming from the stalk but when as it went deeper into the ground the roots got thicker and thicker.

It was here that I found my greatest discovery, a creature that blurs the lines between animal and plant.

I found it when I was observing a Dragonfly trying to decide if it was the same as the ones on earth, but when it landed on a leaf, the plant closed with a snap then I saw the stalk swallow the bug like a snake, then the leaf slowly opened again like a Venus flytrap on earth.

Then the ground and dirt went up like plume and the plant started to move, then from beyond the bushes a creature the size of Ringo strolled out into the open, the creature looked like a small completely brown lizard with three sharp claws on its four feet and a straight cone like tail on it rear end, but instead of a head its neck hole had three plants growing from it, each had a normal looking leaf that was flexible to close on prey and swallow it whole, all facing a different direction.

I looked for eyes but couldn't see any, it was as I stepped closer to the creature that I notice just behind and slightly above, growing from the same stalk and each of its leaf-mouths is a small black bulb looking thing with a small white dot in each one, these must be the eyes as when one of the white dots face me, made a squeal and started to somewhat run around.

I tried to follow but as I did I was hit by a blast of wind with the force of an old electric fan, (like the ones in the museums), placed right next to the face, while on full blast. The source of the wind was a moth the size of an earth seagull flying past me. I must have disturbed it when walking past, the Moth had dark blue and red wings with yellow circles on them like eyes staring at you, as if straight into your soul.

After a few more hours walking and exploring I came across a bush full of small berries, I looked at them, I considered if they might be poisonous?

I decided to grab a few, put them into my pocket to try, or not I haven't decided if to risk it.

As the day grew late I thought I must go back to camp, but a part of me wanted to continue searching, but ignoring my curiosity I reluctantly turned back.

I entered camp just when darkness fell, I first put the berries I collected in to the cave near to the meat, I then walk out and sat down by the burnt-out fire watching the smoke billow up into the sky, and feeling at ease I laid down and fell asleep, with the thought of what other wonders are around on this planet streaming through my mind.

Day 14

The next morning I carved a leg off the body of the Lion-hog and, (after cooking it), shared it with Ringo.

Then half way through eating the skies turn black and a raging thunderstorm struck, like the one that destroyed the ship, taking place just a few miles away. I saw the lightning strike down nearby trees in the direction of where I was only yesterday.

I then started to worry for the creatures that lived in that forest, hoping that they were either far away from the strikes, or has some kind of shelter.

But then worrying about Ringo and myself, I pick up Ringo with one hand and the other holding onto the food I'd cooked, rushed deep into the cave and waited out the storm.

After about what felt like hours, within the darkness of the cave with the only light shining from outside, a small squat figure came walking in.

When it smelt the ground it seem to pick up my scent, as it came straight towards me.

It was only when it got close enough I noticed it was the growler that camped with me the other night, as I notice the three toes on its feet.

When it came closer it sat next to me, and slowly kept inching its way over, with a huge crash of thunder the creature jumped into my lap next to Ringo and buried its head into my body like a scared child.

I held them both tightly and we all sat together in the shadows of the cave.

After about four or five hours the storm stopped, but to make sure we wasn't in the eye we stayed put for what felt like forever, but was probably another hour.

When I was certain that it was safe outside I lead the way out of the cave with Ringo on my shoulder as normal and the Growler waddling slowly behind me, and a Rabbit corpse in hand ready to cook for my supper.

As we got outside, Ringo jumped off my shoulder and started to run in circles with what I can only assume as happiness, and the Growler ran with a wobble towards the campfire, which was now wet as sand in the ocean, and sat patiently like a child waiting to see a school principle. It seemed he was waiting for me to start the fire and maybe waiting to share my meal with him.

So with the Growler waiting, Ringo finally settling down nearby and with my stomach needing food, I prepared the rabbit like normal. As there was no offal for Ringo, I cooked the meat and shared it between all three of us, I was the first to finish with Ringo second, and the Growler took his time nibbling the meat slowly.

After we were done, and the night grew on I laid down near the fire looking up at the night sky and starting to think of home, as tears came to my eyes Ringo and the Growler came up to me and seemed to try and comfort me. Ringo lick my hand while laying on my chest and the Growler digging his head into my side and sat next to me.

After about ten minutes both of my friends fell asleep and I lay there for a while with the thought of my newly found friends in my head,

"I can't leave these two behind when I go home" I whispered to myself as I fell asleep.

Day 15

The next morning when I woke up, and noticed the Growler was sitting by the fire again.

I walked up to him and petted his head, which he seemed to love, and I decided to name him Podge, he looked up at me when I said his name and seemed to purr like a Cat. I went into the cave grabbed the rag that was my old shirt and tore more of it to make a new collar and took the last leg of the Lion-hog for breakfast.

When I emerged from the cave I put the food on the makeshift pit, which I had to remake last night after the storm, and lit the fire. While it was cooking I took the collar and wrapped it around his leg, as he had no neck, which he didn't seem to mind.

Going back to the cooking of the meat on the spit, I heard a screech in the sky and looked up and saw a huge bird coming straight towards the camp.

The bird swooped down and tried to grab Ringo from the ground, the bird looked like an Eagle on earth, but had blue feathers and a bright red crest on its head.

Ringo with fright scurried towards me for protection, as the bird tried again, I jump and covered my friend with my own body, then the bird landed on my back and tried to peck Ringo's tail, I tried to push his tail under me or cover it up, but it kept poking out for the bird to peck.

I shouted to Podge to get away when he waddled

to me, but instead he jumped and grabbed the bird's tail with his mouth. The bird screeched with pain and tried to fly away, but Podge's weight held the bird down and using his little arms, Podge slowly devoured the bird, the bird tried to peck him to make him let go but Podge must have very thick skin for it didn't seem to affect him or even penetrate his round body or thick legs. The gory mess was horrific, but at the same time I was glad and grateful for Podge's help.

I sat up and checked Ringo's tail for any wounds, but luckily his fur was the only thing damaged. I laughed looking at the bald patch on Ringo's tail, and sat back with relief looking at Podge then Ringo.

As the day went on I noticed, upon carving meat for lunch, I realised that my supplies are dwindling, I have not been hunting much recently.

My heart sank at the thought of this constant hunt for survival, this is my life until I get rescued, if I get rescued, that sudden thought sickened me.

It was at this point I got very depressed about the constant killing, but I knew this is what I have to do to survive.

Later that afternoon I set out with a makeshift spear, that I'd made previously during lunch, constructed with a branch from a nearby tree, for my next kill I would be leaving my friends at the camp. I travelled thought the trees nearby, creeping slowly for about half a mile hoping, and waiting for my prey.

I sat for what felt like half an hour, crouched at the ready for some sort of creature, it was then I heard a crack deep in the forest, as it seemed to get closer I readied myself for the kill.

After ten minutes or so I saw my prey, it looked like a Wolf but had ears like a Rabbit and had two long fangs like a Vampire within a long thick snout. It didn't notice me as it walk by approximately fifteen yards from my location.

I crept slowly towards it, spear in hand ready to kill, as the Rabby-wolf sniffed the ground it turned and looked in my direction, knowing that this has gone very wrong I stood still hoping he wouldn't noticed me, but I was wrong. The creature charged straight towards me, growling and snarling with bloodlust in its eyes.

As the Wolf leapt at me I readied my spear and struck the brute in the chest and blood started to pour from the wound and down the spear, as the Wolf wailed in pain he fell to the ground and the spear snapping as it did so.

Knowing I lost my weapon and the Rabby-wolf was still alive. With blood oozing from the wound, the wolf seemed to weaken, it was still angry and alive. I had no choice but to run, which was a big mistake, for it seemed to make the beast not only angrier but also made it a challenge to kill me, for as I took off running the Rabby-wolf seemed to put its pain aside and chased after me. Luckily, the wound slowed him down just enough for me to have time to climb a tree and prepare myself for combat. As the Wolf circled the tree waiting for me, for a few moments I started to laugh, not sure why, I could be going mad but it seemed like the last few minutes was like something from a book.

Pushing that thought aside I broke of branches for more weapons to use, but to no avail, the branches were useless for throwing but I did find one that I could use as a dagger as it snapped of in a jagged fashion, now I had the problem of how to stab at it without my face being torn off. It didn't help that the day was entering twilight and I knew I hadn't long to kill the beast and take it back to camp.

I decided, as I had no choice I held the short, sharp sturdy branch tightly, and timing it right I jumped out of the tree and onto the back of the beast. I brought down the beast with the force of my body landing on him I quickly stabbed it in the head not once but three times, with each stab the Wolf yelped and after the third the wolf fell to the ground looking at me with tired eyes. I grabbed the makeshift dagger and stabbed the Rabby-wolf one last time though the side of his head killing it instantly.

Then with regret in my heart I hugged the body of the beast and I cried with such despair in my mind, as the tears stream down my face I was constantly saying not only sorry to the creature, but I also thanked it for its sacrifice.

With tears still stinging my eyes I dragged the beast back to camp, I got back late in the night, as I entered camp both Ringo and Podge sat quietly waiting for my return.

I dragged the carcass in to the cave's cold interior, and strolled back out, it was then that Ringo and Podge both came to me and seemed to try and comfort me, as if they knew I was upset. I hugged them tightly with happiness for their company and love.

After a while of constant replaying the events of the day in my mind I fell asleep with dreams of going home and never leaving earth again.

Day 16

I awoke before the sun rose and before both Ringo and Podge awoke; although they stirred when I walked pass them to the edge of camp.

As I looked around, I felt despair, I was hoping the past fifteen days where nothing more than a deep coma sleep, and I was safely back on earth with my wife next to me.

In my deepening sadness and self-pity, I realised I had something to feel happiness about; I had Ringo and Podge to keep me company and protect. I needed them more than ever.

I looked up at the sky, watching the stars fade by the coming sun and part of my fear faded with it.

I started to prepare food like I had done every day and waited for my friends to awaken, after an hour or so of sunlight Podge woke up and Ringo shortly after. The food was done and I shared it between us.

While eating I sneezed and coughed, and I realised I may have some sort of illness, my heart sank at this revelation for I could die from it, after all this is an alien world and must have some kind of alien bacteria.

I tried to ignore the thought, but from that moment the worry was always there, growing and festering in the back of my mind ready to constantly invade my waking thoughts and bring me down in the dark depths of sorrow.

It was at this point I came to the realisation; I must explore this world and keep my mind active, so there is no time for my mind to wallow in pity and sadness.

After we had all done eating, Ringo jumped on my shoulder and made himself comfy before I had any time to say no and Podge readied himself by my legs, it seemed they were wanting to go with me, maybe for company, but I could not be sure.

I went east from camp to find new plants and animal, on my search I had Podge following behind me, and Ringo napping on my shoulder.

Exploring the surrounding forest I discovered more new plants. One of them had a stem about a foot long, large leaves that looked like two-inch by two-inch green diamonds. The stem had two or three of them and the head of the plant had four long, slender petals of pink and the middle was a bright yellow, I dug up one of these plants and the root system was interesting, instead of a complex set of strands digging deep into the dirt it had only two thick, long stems penetrating the ground like a two-pronged fork, it looked as if the stem was split in half for the roots.

Another plant had a bell shape flower with purple petals; the long green stem grew darker the closer it neared the ground.

Off the main stem grew a second, on it where hard pebble-like growths, they look like berries but hard as stone, I theorize that maybe this pebbles are actually some kind of seed, ready to break away from the plant and roll with the wind to some new area to grow, or they explode releasing the seeds inside where they would float

on the breeze to go elsewhere to grow, either way it is fascinating.

I dug up one and found very strange roots, it had one long growth that was like the spiral of a Seahorse's tail, the darken stem just above the ground became jet black underground, plus the tip of the root was some kind of strand similar to that of human hair which spiralled opposite to the root itself.

I dug up three more of these plants from nearby, to check the roots for the same unique root system like that of the first, my findings were this type of plant had all the same roots and for this reason I called this plant the Seahorse bell.

When digging these up Ringo just continued to nap on my shoulder, while Podge sat quietly watching. Then needing to do some business behind a tree. A thought came to me out of nowhere, when do both Ringo and Podge take a dump, I have never seen them do so, and a question race though my mind,

"Do they crap away from camp when I'm not near? I bloody well hope so".

For if Podge took a dump near camp you would smell it from a mile away, but then it came to me no other animals came near my camp, since Podge had settled with me. Before that night I saw other animal and sounds around camp, then Podge came and nothing, this made me think is Growler faeces some kind of deterrent for other creatures so they won't go near their home?

Then I thought about Ringo, and I thought about the amount of time he sleeps on my shoulders that he must just poop when he feels like it, which means on me, and my first thought was "yuck", but I couldn't tell him off, after all he helps me when I need it and he is wild. But still "yuck".

I continued my exploration and found an insect unlike any that I'd seen on earth, I was the size of an average human hand with six wings, three on each side, about thirty centimetres long and each looked see-through and like a tear drop from a child's drawing.

The body was in two jet-black parts like an ant without a head, the larger of which seemed like the main body and the head all in one with the smaller maybe holding the organs like most insects? This I may never know unless I could catch one for study, for which I am not equipped.

All I know is that what I believe is the mouth was very prominent and looked like a beak with two lower jaw hook mandibles and this was on the larger body part and seem to walk with the beak leading the way, (unless it has a weird, shaped butt and walks backwards for some reason).

The legs were like six sticks about two inches long and attached on the larger of the two body pieces and seem to not be able to bend, but each one has an extremely large claw that it would use to dig into and to keep attached to things, in this case a tree.

The colour of the bug, at closer inspection, wasn't black, but was actually a very dark green and only noticeable when I walked closer, and the light hit it right.

I also noticed the antenna of the bug were also like long sticks and only moved slightly.

I tried to get closer but the insect flew away, as it did so the buzzing was very loud for an insect and very fast, so I came to the conclusion that it must fly more than walk hence the stick like legs and the large wings.

I tried to walk on and explore more, but I started to sneeze and cough more and more so I decided to walk back to try and tend to my oncoming illness.

It was early evening when I got back to camp, and by that time my unknown sickness took hold of me more and more.

Every time I coughed the rougher my throat felt and by the time twilight set in, it was hard to swallow anything, even water, it felt like tiny needles making their way down my throat, my sinus felt like it was easing off at first but then it started to sting just breathing though it. Then after a while my nose was so stuffed up it was impossible to breath.

I decided to give Ringo and Podge food, and I have an early night to fight the virus off, and I hoped it was just a common cold.

Then as I was drifting off, I worried about Ringo and Podge, for if this is an Earth virus will they be all right? I then hope it was a virus from this planet similar to a cold and I could fight it off and Ringo and Podge would be ok.

Day 17

I awoke with such a terrible headache that I knew I couldn't go exploring today, it was then I started to miss Dr Monroe. The thought surprised me and at the same time felt wrong, for if he was here, he would take the piss while I'm in pain and then I would have the urge to punch him, but couldn't as he is a doctor and I would need his medical advice. I don't think he would tell me if I hit him, it would have been fun though. So, instead I would call him a pompous ass and then he would tell me the diagnosis after giving me the finger and calling me an ungrateful shit and all would be well.

So with a headache, which made my head feel like a heavy rock, I prepare food for Ringo, Podge and myself.

After having breakfast, I lay back and relaxed and started to nap and try to sleep off my illness. Podge snuggled up by my side and Ringo made himself comfy on my stomach and we all napped in the light of the morning sun.

After about two hours I felt Podge walk away and came back after half hour or so, I think he went to crap, Ringo did the same an hour or so later, maybe to do the same?

After a few hours' sleep I awoke, to the sound of shrieking from the cave, like tiny dogs fighting over food.

I picked up Ringo carefully and placed him next to

Podge so not to disturb them and went to investigate the sounds alone.

As I entered the shadows, I had a thoughts of terrible things of which I hope I'll never see.

"This could be nothing more than a rat," I whispered to myself trying to calm my nerves.

When I got to the main area of the cave all I heard was the sound of the running water,

"Am I going insane?" I asked myself with worry. I then turned to walk out of the gloominess of the cave, but then I heard the shrieking sound again. The sound came from the food I collected and with my heart beating faster than ever; I inched my way over to the noise trying not to make a sound.

As I looked over the rock to check my food supplies, there was nothing there, I looked around the food and found nothing.

I turn to walk away and it hit me, there was a small bite mark on the body of the Rabby-wolf.

I started to think my illness had got to me, for the bite look like a small human bite, but with many sharp fangs, looking at it put a terror in my heart like never before, my veins felt as if an injection of fire had been taken into my body and my heart started to beat uncontrollably.

It was at this point I began to feel tired, my childhood coping mechanism struck me again, or it could just be my illness playing with my head, then I thought maybe this whole experience could be nothing more than my delusional ill mind making me see and hear things.

I knew I had to look for the creature, delusion or not, for not only my own curiosity, but also safety, not only me but for Ringo and Podge.

So with panic in my mind and fear slowing my movements, I tried to find the thing before it attacked.

It was at this point I wished the security officer Malcolm Wingard from the ship had survived, if he was here he would start searching not stop, the man was like a machine when danger was near. It was like when a danger switch was present in his brain, when trouble was about it would flip on from and the nice guy that you could have a laugh with, would turn into some sort of robot warrior, eager for the kill and disperse the danger.

Alas I am alone, and I will not put Ringo or Podge in danger, so I continue my search.

I started by going to the entrance of the cave and making a sweep of the area hoping to find the creature and trap him inside and hoping to see if it tries to escape.

As I started the search, the clouds outside covered up the sun, so less light came into the cave making it harder to see in the darkness, my own shadow hindering me more.

I accidentally struck my foot on a largish rock hurting my toe and bending my nail slightly backwards inside my shoe. I then began to shout and cursing like a sailor, I heard a strange laughing sound like some sort of imp finding my pain funny, was this a delusion I wondered, either way this made my angry soar and my fear slightly diminish.

So with a new boost to my morale I challenged the Imp to show itself, I felt stupid almost instantly, thinking that the thing won't even know what I'm saying, but my foolishness paid off for the Imp did show itself just for an instant then disappeared back into the darkness. Just long enough for me to see it.

What I saw of the creature was amazing, it did look like an Imp or Gnome from a fairy tale, it had a tiny body like a human with what looked like thick hair on its chest and groin, from what I saw it was male, and had five tiny fingers with what appeared to be sharp talon-like nails and toes. But in this darkness I could be wrong, I couldn't make out skin colour but it seemed greenish-black but again I could be wrong. The face was long with a pronounced pointy chin and a round head with long greasy looking hair, and I must be delusional because all I thought was he need to wash it. His nose was round and bulbous, the eyes where dark and wide, I couldn't see the eye colour in the darkness but something told me they were jet-black. I couldn't see if the Imp had whites of the eyes like humans because of the distance and darkness of the cave.

After the sighting I kept wondering if my mind is playing tricks on me, after all I am ill from maybe an alien illness, this could just be part of it.

But even thought this was a possibility, something inside me told me it was real and I must be very careful.

I looked around in the murky darkness slowly for the annoying creature, I couldn't see it but from deep within the shadows I heard its cackling laugh, the sound seemed to move around the dark cave, it was like the Imp teleported but I knew this could not be.

After the sound of the laughing died down I waited a few minutes for the Imp to return, but he had seemed to have gone, this started to make me think maybe I was wrong and that the Imp was part of my delusional ill mind, which I think is me being hopeful.

It was at this point the headache took a grip of my brain, it felt like my head was going to explode, an ache started to spread over my body as I stumbled out of the cave and back to camp.

When I returned I found Ringo sitting waiting by the burnt-out fire and Podge was just coming back to camp from the brush, (maybe he had a dump, I don't know and to be honest I didn't want to check).

I lay back down to rest my aches and pains and Ringo and Podge sat with me like a couple of concerned family members.

I slept for an hour or so when it started to rain then a thunderstorm set in. The storm came from nowhere and I quickly rushed to the cave holding both Ringo and Podge.

When we got into the cave I suddenly remembered the Imp, and was sure I heard the giggling of the crazy monster, but looking at Ringo and Podge they were looking outside the cave watching the lighting not seeming to hear the laughter.

At this point I started to think I was very ill and was hallucinating, so I sat down with my eyes fixated on the deep part of cave just where I had seen the Imp before, just in case. I slowly fell asleep with the Imp fixed firmly in my mind plaguing my sleep.

Day 18

I had horrid nightmares all night, of Imps coming from the cave and attacking all three of us, it started with Ringo, a group of Imps grabbed him by the tale and dragged him inside the cave and all I heard was the screeches of pain as they ripped him apart, the horrid part was I was awake, but couldn't help.

They then did the same to Podge and again I couldn't help, then they came for me, the group covered my body and used their talon like claws and kept scratching me drawing blood, slowly tearing though my flesh and I was powerless to defend myself, then one of the beasts looked me in the eye and raked his talons across my throat, I tried to scream but was unable to, this was when I awoke in a cold sweat.

As I did so I found both Ringo and Podge safe, both asleep by my side, the storm was still raging and I still felt ill but slightly better than yesterday.

So by I now I needed food I ventured into the cold depths of the cave to carve a piece of my supply.

I started to move slowly and found something shocking, a tiny leg just like that from the Imp I had seen.

I picked it up to check to see if it was real or just my mind playing more tricks, but as I felt the cold flesh and saw the bones and blood I knew I was not going mad, either that or my mind is playing a bloody good trick on me.

With the leg in hand I walked back to the cave mouth to see it in daylight, when I got there Podge was awake sitting quietly with his hands folded, waiting.

I examined the leg in the light and it did have a greenish-black skin tone, as I held it up by the foot to count the toes, Podge suddenly jumped and devoured the leg with one gulp, he must of thought it was me giving him food, it was when he opened his mouth to burp I noticed he had a large piece of greenish-black flesh stuck between his fangs, I thought it could be from the leg, but I realised he swallowed that whole somehow, so logic dictates that he ate more than the leg. Which was a relief to me.

The conclusion I came to is the following. Sometime in the night Podge must have heard a noise from the cave and went to investigate, while in the cave he met with the Imp, (that really did exist), and ate it leaving the leg behind in the gruesome struggle.

I couldn't help but laugh at the thought, at the same time was kind of disappointed at the idea that I couldn't study the Imp, but at least I don't have to worry about the danger every time I need water or when I need to collect food.

Know I couldn't do any more today, I prepare some meat and we all had a drink of water and I finally fell asleep and rested.

Day 19

Stuck in the cave with rain pouring and thunder rumbling outside, I tried to keep active doing some exercises, but my illness seemed to come back with a vengeance.

I prepare the last of the food ration, removing pieces for Podge to eat raw, (which he seemed to like better), then cooking the rest for Ringo and myself.

After we had finished eating, with nothing else to do and being stuck inside, I decided to look around the cave closely to check for small passages, where the Imp could have snuck in, then I could block them up to stop further intruders.

As we walked along the passage towards the inner sanctuary of the cave, Podge suddenly ran back to the entrance. Thinking there was something deep inside I too with Ringo on my shoulder ran following Podge back to the entrance.

This is where I felt like a fool, Podge ran out the cave in the rain and thunder, thinking there was something really bad in the cave I ran out also and got completely drenched and started to get worried about getting struck by lightning as we ran towards the trees, and what was all this was for, so Podge could have a shit.

This not only annoyed me, but could also make my ills worst, but I couldn't yell at Podge, he was only doing what is natural, no matter how annoying it is. After he was done and we ran from the smell, (thankfully the rain dampened the stench).

As we got back to the cave, Podge look up at me, all I could say as I looked in his wide bulbous eyes, (that seemed to be filled with the look of, "I'm sorry"), was "Don't do that again", after I said that Podge started to brush himself up against my leg, like a cat after attention and staking his claim.

So back at the cave and completely wet from head to toe, I decided to try and explore the cave once again.

As we got in the inner sanctuary, I lit a small fire with some dry pieces of wood I had found then I removed my wet jacket and decided to put over me the pelt of the Lion-hog that I saved from the carcass, luckily there was no blood on it, it either must have dried or dissipated, it was quite stiff and rough but I don't care it just felt good to get out of the jacket that I wore for the past eighteen days. Plus it was only when I took it off I noticed that it had a tear in the under arm, so I decided to tear of the sleeve completely for scrap.

Within the flickering light of the fire, I searched the cave and found no small openings, so I surmised that Imp must have crept in when we was exploring some time and made himself at home.

After finding no irregularities, I decided to try to sleep for the rest of the day to try and fight off my illness and with my new pelt I felt quite warm even within the chilly inner cave.

It took a few hours to get to sleep, my mind kept worrying if more Imps trespassed into this cave I called home. But the thought of being back home, with my wife safe and with Ringo and Podge in tow, thinking this for a few minutes I easily drifted off to sleep.

Day 20

The next morning the storm had passed and I felt a lot better, my illness whatever it was is nearly gone, all I have are the sniffles and a dry throat.

Ringo was in fine form also this morning, running in circles actively around like a hamster would on a running wheel.

Podge was a bit tired it seemed, walking a few steps then closing his eyes and resting for a few moments.

I started to worry that Podge may have caught something off me, but this worry was quashed in seconds as a roaring sound similar to that of a large balloon deflating came from the embarrassed looking Podge.

And the smell, of a burst sewage pipe, invaded the area and into nostrils of Ringo and me, it made my eyes water, (I'm not sure about Ringo's eyes). Podge started to run around me like an excited child with not a care in the world, even after gassing the area.

To escape the stink, the three of us went wandering around the area; we started to walk fast to get away from the area. Then when the smell seemed to dissipate we slowed down and when the smell was near enough gone, we sat down to gather our breath.

It was at this point I noticed a peculiar creature strolling by, it had the legs similar to that of a Horse for they were long and slender with bony knees and ankles, they also have hooves that looked to be the same as Horses have on earth. They gave the same sound, I always found that noise relaxing.

The body of the beast was a fusion of a Giraffe and a Horse as it had the shape of the Giraffe, but was smaller, plumper and muscular like a Horse.

The rear end was like that of the Growler, but more obvious, this makes me question if this trait was a common occurrence on this planet.

The head of the creature was the long shape of a Horse but with a Fox or Cat-like mouth and nose with what looked like whiskers. Its eyes look cunning like a Fox, but were jet-black with absolutely no whites of the eyes from what I could see. They reminded me of my teddy bear toy I had when I was six.

As I moved, the Hox as I called it, suddenly started to snarl like an angry Dog, and I tried to move slowly away, the Hox just watched with keen eyes, studying my every movement.

Then the Hox started to charge at me, I turned away and made a run for camp knowing I probably wouldn't make it if the Hox were as fast as a Horse on earth.

As the three of us tried to run for camp, (I say three of us, it was more like two as Ringo sat on my shoulder the whole time), the stench of Podge's rectal gas still in the area again invaded my nose, knowing I couldn't stop I pressed on winding our way though the trees like a slithering snake, this slowed down the Hox, for it seem it was fast running in straight lines but not great at turning.

As the stench got thicker the Hox suddenly stopped, I turned to check it and hid behind a tree to catch my breath, (which was hard because of the smell), and then the Hox sniffed the air and yelp as it ran away from the three of us. I looked down at Podge, he looked at me with pride like, "yep that's my gas" sort of pride.

So standing around just outside of camp with the smell of methane in the air, I debated on whether to go out hunting, then I just started to stroll back to camp I wondered if the Hox is out there ready to chase me again and who knows maybe the thing is a carnivore.

While pondering on the situation, the high-pitched sound of a flock of birds, echoed over our heads, I looked up I realised I was right, a flock of birds just like the ones that attacked Ringo and was eaten by Podge.

Knowing this will be a lot worse than last time and seeing they were primed to attack, I made a run for the cave, grabbing Ringo on the way and hiding him tightly under my pelt poncho and Podge running by my side.

As I ran though the few trees into the clearing that was camp. I looked up at the flock that was flying above us, one of the birds decided to make the first strike and swooped down to attack, I didn't see much of the bird due to the fact I had to dodge, all I saw was the beak that was similar to a vulture shining in the light, then I ducked and saw the mass of dark coloured feathers passing overhead and the two slender tails trailing behind the mass. Then a second bird did the same, this one didn't make it for as it got close, Podge grabbed the tail and devoured it like he did with the one from days ago except this time he ran and ate at the same time, though the other birds flew overhead they didn't attack again maybe they saw what happen and thought better off it and decided to wait for Podge to leave.

When I got to the cave we dashed in before another bird could try and dive-bomb us.

The flock flew around in circles for a few minutes then perched on the trees around camp, I felt like I ran for miles but it wasn't far from where we were and I wondered if maybe my illness was still in my system.

I looked out at the flock of birds hanging around, (and still not able to see them clearly), and all I could think was "I saw this movie, it didn't end well".

Day 21

I'm telling anyone who reads this, being stuck in a cave with a flock of carnivorous birds outside waiting to dive-bomb anything that move outside, is no fun.

Especially when you've not had anything to eat, (well except Podge, who had blood around his mouth with feathers stuck to it while every time he burps, more feathers came flying out, Ringo chased the feathers as they fell to the ground).

Then with the feelings of anxiety churning my insides, the stale air making it harder to breath with every second, the sensation of being confined and my mind playing tricks on me, like the walls closing in and being unable to stroll out of the cave into the cool breeze and open space. All this goes around in my mind again and again to the point where I was going to shout and run out with no concern to my own safety, it was then I had to escape from my captivity.

Even now I don't understand why I felt like this, after all I was trapped in the ship for days, and in this very same cave during the storm for longer, but for some reason this felt worse. I then think maybe it was due to being confined against my will, just maybe.

To escape I first tried simple techniques, I grabbed the largest rock I could throw and went to the cave mouth and threw it like a soldier would lob a grenade at his enemy.

The result was as unexpected as it was annoying, the flock in unison leaned out of the way calmly like they had some sort of hive-mind.

I really thought that the bloody creatures would bugger off with a large rock coming at them, but with the things acting calm I suddenly lost it, I burst out the cave, red with anger shouting and screaming such profanity at the creatures that even a group of hardy and experience sailors would blush.

The weird thing was, this actually scared the flock of birds away a lot quicker than I could imagine and all I could say in such bewilderment was

"Huh."

So with my newfound freedom, I decided to go hunting for yet another supply of food.

I told Podge to guard camp and Ringo to stay with Podge; they seemed to understand what I was saying, for they didn't follow me.

So as I strolled away from camp with Podge watching me from in front of the cave and Ringo asleep by his side. I went alone into the forest for some food; the annoying thing was I had no weapon so I had to rely on my human cunning and resourcefulness.

It didn't take long to find a Rabbit hopping along though the trees, I followed the creature for a few yards to strike at the perfect time. When suddenly a Hox, very similar looking to the one I saw before, trampled over the Rabbit like a Horse, stopped quickly with a slight slide, he turned back to the injured Rabbit and stomped on the poor things neck. A loud crunch echoed through the area and I turned to get away, then suddenly I heard the sound of snarling behind me, as I turn I saw the Hox angry looking face up close, the scene was something like that from a horror movie.

I tried to back away slowly, not breaking eye contact. I was a few yards away; I made a run for camp winding my way through the trees like a serpent once again to dodge the Hox.

When I saw the edge of camp I noticed Podge asleep where I had left him with Ringo still by his side, I then realised where I was leading the Hox at the last moment I made a very sharp 180 degrees turn, this made the Hox slip on the mud badly, sliding into camp, Ringo then awoke and ran away quickly while Podge kept snoozing, the Hox then tripped on the sleeping Podge and fell badly breaking its own neck and dying instantly, Podge didn't even notice that something hit him.

As I walked up to the dead creature, after waking and checking Podge to see if he was ok, all I could think about was karma was a bitch, this creature broke the neck of the Rabbit, then breaking its own, weird.

I dragged the body into the cold depths of the cave, and walk back into the forest and bringing back the body of the Rabbit for supper, as I always say, "Waste not, want not".

After preparing the meat and dividing it into three equal portions, we all devoured the meat like starving Tigers. When we were all finished, I laid down looking up at the stars as twilight turned to darkness, with Ringo on my stomach and Podge by my side, I wondered about, how much they both sleep. Then watching the stars I drifted off to sleep myself.

Day 22

I awoke, once again knowing that I was still stranded with no help on the horizon, I decided to try and learn more of the strange unpopulated world I find myself on.

I set off early leaving Podge and Ringo asleep by the cave entrance.

I just hoped that they wouldn't awake and think I abandon then.

I walked southeast from the cave, leaving markers on the trees to guide me back. After a while or so I decided to rest and note some of the local flora, most of which looked similar to that which is on earth but with some notable exceptions.

One of which looked like a tall lavender flower, with small white buds populating the main stem. The buds looked as if they haven't yet bloomed which leads me to the conclusion that either I crashed during this planets summer or autumn seasons or this world has no proper seasons, so that flowers bloom whenever the time comes rain or shine.

As I stared at the plant taking notes, a small pebble hit me in the back of my head, I looked around with fear in my heart imagining some kind of human-like tribe ready to kill trespassers. But there was nothing behind me. Then again was pelted with yet another pebble, this time with some force, in the exact same position on the back of my head. I felt I was being mess with by some strange force and decided it would be best if I slinked away before it gets worst.

As I turn towards camp I was pelt three more times by pebbles and small rocks, it was at this time I dash away from my unknown enemy. After two or three yards a figure appeared from the overhanging tree branch, I tried to stop and avoid hitting the unknown beast, slipping and falling down doing so. As I regained my standing I came face to face with an unusual type of monkey-like creature, it appeared to have soft purple fur with cute wide eyes and paw like that of a dog. The most peculiar aspect of the beast was the large ears, each the size of seven-inch plate.

After a few moments staring are each other as if we're having some kind of contest, I decided to step a little further. As I raised my hand to pet the beast the monkey completely change, it's eyes narrowed and blackened, fluffy paws became sharp bladed claws, it's fuzzy face became mad and angry displaying a fine set of fangs and its ears produced tiny bony spikes protruding from around the ears circumference. Suddenly it growled like a bobcat, leaving me speechless and shaking.

The worst part of the encounter was that every time I moved to try and escape, it mimicked my movement. I know the only way to get away was to dash for the camp and the safety of Podge that would most likely, eat such a creature.

After counting to three, I made a mad dash for camp with the creepy simian giving chase; keep up with every move I made. After five minutes of running I started to tire, I put this down to the lack of proper nutrition and decided to stand my ground face to face again with the crazy chimp. I stood prepare for a fight I may lose when suddenly a blue blur past my head and the chimp was gone, I look around bewildered only to see the chimp struggling with a blue coloured serpent. After a few moments of struggling the snake coiled around the monkey as it fought with everything it had, a crack was heard and the monkey went limp.

I noted the serpent as it ate the chimp whole like snakes on earth, unlike earth snakes the serpent looked like the depictions of dragons from China, it was the size of a king cobra, but had two small limbs just like little arms. I pondered if the limbs were a new evolution as this serpent started growing them or was it evolving and losing its limbs instead, ether way it was fascinating. Also unlike earthly snakes it had a lion-like mane, but instead of fur it looked like a porcupine quills.

After it swallowed the chimp it, slowly slithered into a nearby bush and seem to disappear. This I thought strange for such a vibrant blue was able to blend into the flora so quickly. I must come to the conclusion, that it must be able to change it colour pigments to match its surroundings.

At this point the skies darkened and rain began to rapidly fall. I ran back to my camp with notes of new discoveries, new fears. Upon reaching the camp I was extremely exhausted.

Day 23

I thought about the last few weeks as I lay on the ground, while the morning sun rose, and I became homesick as I stared up at the bright blue sky of such a dangerous but at the same time wondrous planet.

I missed home, I missed my books, and my vintage video games, but I really missed my wife.

It felt like hours but as I started to tear up at the thought of home, I looked around and felt grateful I'm not alone.

Suddenly a drone flew overhead awaking both Podge and Ringo, I was overjoyed at seeing the machine I jumped up and shouted for it, then I felt like a right fool as I remember such devices are unmanned.

Then in the midst of the relief, I wondered how did anyone know about us? It should have taken a year for the signal to reach anyone, I pushed this question out of my mind because as long as I get home I don't care.

So knowing the drone has just flown past I knew they must have pick up my internal beacon and traced it back to the ship it came from. I could be rescued in a matter of a day to a week at most.

I first thought of staying here living quietly and wait. But then I thought, what if I explore this world for the last few days and impress the likes of Leon Parker of my new discoveries.

So taking my sketchbook I went out on another mission of exploration.

I left the friendly duo once again at camp as I could live with myself if they got hurt because of any stupid mistakes I most likely will make. I walked north around the cave and into the thicket of foliage, after about an hour or so I came across a small new pond with a pale blue colour and a calming feel.

As I looked in it I could see the water rippling as if something was swimming in it, but I could see nothing.

I decided to try the water, and was disgusted by the taste of salt water; this surprised me for I have never heard of a pond of salt water this far inland, unless I'm near the coast.

Just then as I spat out the water, a splash came from the pond as an unknown creature leapt out like and bullet and attached itself onto my arm.

I looked at the hideous creature and instantly pulled to remove it, but the thing was on tight, I should have tried to kill it, and then remove it, but in my panic I pulled harder.

Eventually the creature was removed and what felt like my skin along with it. As the pain of its removal was intense and stung like a huge needle going through my arm and then slowly being removed.

As I held onto the creature tightly around its slimy fleshy body I realised the skin of the thing was a dark brown, this perplexed me for I should have seen it in the pond as the water was so clear, the overall size of the creature was about 20cm and look like a thick worm, I also noted that it had tentacles that looked like pieces of string, and as they tried to wrap around my hand I theorize that it uses the to attach themselves to its prey.

Its mouth opened and made a squealing sound as it did so, the mouth looked like a four-leaf clover with each leaf connected to each other with a fleshy membrane. On each opening of the mouth was filled with hundreds of tiny fangs lining the mouth entrance and down to the throat and each fang seemed to move independently making its mouth like a tiny shredder.

As it started to struggle I threw it back into the water, after about a few seconds it seemed to change its skin colour to match the water, this must be why I didn't see it straight away, it had camouflage, the bastard.

Then as I walked away of the pond I wondered, as I couldn't see any other fish in the pond does it eat flesh or only blood; going by the way it latched itself onto me I'd say it eats flesh.

Five minutes of walking I felt something steaming down my arm, I then realised the severity of my wound and found something shocking. Where the creature was removed it not only removed the first layer of skin, but also parts of the muscle in my arm to the point that I could just see my bone.

After seeing the wound I then began to feel the pain, it shot though my arm to my torso and into my brain. I slowly walk back to camp holding myself up on the trees along the way, the pain made me dizzy and sick but somehow I made my way back.

When I enter camp Ringo and Podge both ran to me and seem to try and help me as I crawled on my knees and my one good arm slowly I my way into the cave. When I reached the inner chamber, I crawled to the spare rags of my old jacket I looked at the wound and realised it was worse then I thought I grabbed one of the spare pieces of cloth to wrap around my arm tightly, to try and stop the bleeding, as I did so I felt such pain that I fell to the ground and passed out with one thought going through my mind "Oh shit".

Day 24

Upon awakening, a strong dull pain shot up and down my arm and running into my body like some sort of acid in my blood stream.

As I examined my makeshift bandage, I was shocked to find blood seeping through and dripping onto not only the floor, but also all over my fur poncho.

"I'm a bloody idiot," I repeated to myself over and over again as I started to remove the bandage and replace it with another rag,

"Oh shit!" I said with worry and surprised, I could see the bone within my own arm only a tiny bit but still.

"I'm a bloody moron" I started to repeat to myself seeing the extent of my injury.

The only thing I was happy about is that part of the bloody gory hole in my arm was starting to clot, still every time I thought of it all I could say to myself was, "Blood hell" with for some reason, which I cannot fathom, it sounded like I had an Australian accent.

When I had finally finished sorting out my arm I noticed I only had two more rags I could use. So, I decided to stay at camp until rescue, I also noticed Ringo and Podge were not present, I didn't really worry for it was early morning and they maybe outside around the camp playing or out for "toilet" time.

As I stumbled out of the cave, suddenly feeling very

weak, when I got close to the burnt-out fire I sat, (or should I say collapse), by the embers to rest.

As I looked around the camp I realised it was empty with no sign of the duo anywhere or any sign where they may be.

I still wasn't worried for they may be out for the morning wander.

But after about an hour I then started to worry about the duo and I thought I should look for them both, but as I stood I suddenly felt extremely dizzy and fell back down.

I then decided to myself that I would wait for another ten minutes, after that I would search for them dizzy of not.

Ten minutes went by so I tried to stand once more with the same result, I then began to worry more having no idea what to do,

"I can't leave them," I whispered to myself, "but I can barely stand."

Suddenly a rustling of a bush announced the return of Podge waddling back to camp with Ringo sitting on his head enjoying the ride, they both were holding a bunch of Rats, (well Podge was holding them in his arms, Ringo had two in his mouth like a cat proud of his catch), as they saw me, Podge suddenly ran towards me, Ringo fell of his head and as he fell to the ground, he looked around shocked, righted himself then ran towards me also.

When they both reached me they both began to either nuzzle me or lick me like a Dog might with his owner, they seem to be happy to see me as if they were worried about me being hurt.

When they were done they remembered the Rats and

placed them in front of me I counted six, I thanked them and lit a new fire to cook them.

After I put the food on the spit, Ringo and Podge started to act like carers, for the rest of the day they brought me things to try and help my recovery, Podge brought me water in the skull I used for cleaning, I just hope it is safe to drink from, but as it only held fresh water, it should be fine. And Podge even understood when the food was done cooking he took it from the spit when it was ready, (this proved to me that Podge was intelligent enough to understand cooking). Ringo brought me utensils and small items throughout the day and helped pass me Rats to prepare for Podge to cook.

When darkness fell and Podge and Ringo was asleep, I started to feel an unusual sensation tingling through my arm, it felt like some sort of Worm or other bug moving around the wound through the muscle and into the rest of my arm hitting the nerves as it did so.

I put all this down to my overactive imagination and tired mind.

Then suddenly before I fell asleep I'm sure I heard movement on the edge of camp. It scurried into the long grass, to the bushes and into the trees, I looked at the friendly duo and thought maybe it was only a harmless animal, due to the fact neither Podge or Ringo noticed, I looked in the direction of the noise but after ten or so minutes I decided to put it down to my brain making up things. My imagination was running wild.

Day 25

I awoke to a screeching sound piercing my ears, the sound started with a ringing but then after minutes it shot like fire though the veins into my brain, it felt as if my brain would explode at any moment.

I then started to miss Dr Monroe, not as a person, but as a doctor, he would know what to do not only about the screeching, but also my other ailments.

I then sat up, big mistake for it seem the screeching got louder as I did so, I then lay back down, thinking that it would be better, but instead this made things worse and the sound got even louder.

Over time the pitch of the sound grew in intensity until it reached the point, where I had to try and cover my ears to try and stop the sound.

This didn't work, the sound got to the point where my eardrums, felt like they were going to burst, and then suddenly the screeching stopped.

I looked around to check on the friendly duo, they both seemed fine running around playing like nothing has happened.

It was at this moment I looked at my arm and wondered if my injury has somehow effected my healing, was there some sort of infection going through my blood stream making me hear things.

I was going to check on my arm, when suddenly

from, south of the camp well I think it is. The rustling of the bushes reveal two male Growlers as they jumped out with hunger in their eyes.

Then before you could say "bloody hell", Ringo dashed away from where he and Podge where playing and ran towards me, I was struggling to stand, and he scurried up my legs and body onto my shoulders, while Podge waddled back and hid behind my legs.

The three of us stood just watching the Growlers while they watch back, both groups waiting for the other to make the first move.

Podge then inched his way in front of me and seemed to try and talk to them, the strange sounding grunts and yelps must be some kind of language to them but I could be wrong it might just be sounds of defiance.

In return the "visitors" pounced at Podge with tooth and claw, Podge was able to dodge the attacks and hit one of them knocking it to the ground while the other tripped on his own momentum.

As they both got up and tried to attack Podge once again, I ran towards him to try and protect him while also making loud growling sounds to try and frighten the enemy away.

This didn't work, instead one started to attack me while the other went for Podge, at first they tried to slice and dice me with their claws and then tried to bite me, luckily all the attacks missed as I dodge by jumping back slightly.

Suddenly as I tried to dodge yet another attack, I stumble and fell on my arm, while Ringo rolled of me.

With pain shooting though my arm once again, I tried

to keep focus on Ringo, I saw though my blurred vision of searing pain the Growler charging over to Ringo, most likely because he was smaller and easier target.

When Podge saw this he suddenly ran faster than I have ever seen him run before with anger upon his face, as he got close he roared with such anger.

The roar made the Growlers pause for a moment before they tried to continue their attack, this must have pissed off Podge even more so, like I've never seen before. He readied himself like a sumo wrestler would before a match, stamping his feet on the ground, his hair stood on end like a porcupine and roared like never before.

The sound echoed though out, not only camp, but also through the entire area.

This not only made the Growlers pause, but also run away yelping, like young puppy dogs in terror.

Exhausted, I crawled on my one good arm and knees up to Ringo, Podge was already by his side like a big brother checking his younger sibling, as I got to their side I laid tired, in pain and needing rest.

As I looked up at the sky, I wondered why does everything try to kill Ringo? I thought he needs to be more careful. I also began to wonder why the two male Growlers were working together as I have only seen mating pairs helping each other hunting and had never seen them in groups, I thought maybe they were a mating pair like Humans have different sexualities maybe Growlers have the same. I then decided it wasn't my place to pry as it has nothing to do with me or worry me in anyway.

After the attack I was wondering why do I constantly

feel tired and exhausted, could my wound and the loss of blood have made me anaemic in some way or is it just that such a wound is just making me feel rough? But as it had stopped bleeding shouldn't I feel better?

The rest of the day was totally uneventful and I barely moved from my position from where I lay after the attack, both Ringo and Podge were very helpful trying to feed me throughout the day. I felt a bit like a lazy bastard, because it should be me that cares for the duo.

Day 26

Yet another day on this lonely boring isolated planet full of wonder of which I cannot explore or have the supplies to go any further than a few yards or miles.

Yet again I awake, prepare breakfast, eat and then sit for hours with such mind-numbing boredom, for hours I napped awaking for fifteen-minute intervals.

After lunch, (which was the longest time I was awake during the day), I'd had enough. I had to do something to burn away my tiredness and boredom, so I decided to explore more around camp.

I was just about to leave when my arm started to sting ever so slightly and as I looked at the wound there was a lot oozing slightly making its way through the rag, I removed the make-shift bandage and I noticed long blue veins moving out from my wound stretching out over my arm towards my shoulder and the rest of my body.

Fear went through me like a fire injected into my veins and panic filled my brain and all I could think was, "bloody hell" with the same Australian accent, bizarre.

It was at this point when I started to miss the Doc again, stupid pompous ass he had to die didn't he.

After patching myself up I wondered if I should just wait to be rescued, but after another droll hour, I settled on the idea of exploring.

As I readied myself for the journey I was about to

take, I suddenly noticed the quick movement of some unidentified figure dashing into the nearby brush.

I looked in the direction I'm sure the shadow entered the greenery, then to Ringo and Podge, who were just watching me with their wide eyes.

The duo didn't seem to notice the noise or the movement of the brush, but also the quick shadow running away from camp.

I asked them if they saw anything, they just stared at me erect like soldiers awaiting orders from their commander, but unable to understand as if I was speaking some alien language, which technique I was, but I did' think we understood each other well but apparently not.

In the end I put the movement and sounds to my fear-induced, over-active, bored out of my mind, brain.

So keeping a close eye on the bushes and the surrounding area, I went exploring on the edge of camp.

I was intrigued about finding not only a new plant but also a new creature.

The plant was like an orchid in structure the petals on the flower were a lighter green than its leaves, but with purple edges and tips.

The size was about few inches from the ground, I dug out one of the plants the roots were unremarkable except that the colour was the

same purple as the tips of the leaves.

The new slimy-like creature looked like a slug, I picked it up carefully, (remembering the pond vividly), and studied it for a few moments and noted its eyes that were six black dots and a wide opening mouth. There were tiny tentacles, maybe to pull food towards its mouth for consumption, the overall look of the creature reminded me of a creature from a sci-fi novel.

I was astounded that I missed these finds for days and may have missed them completely especially as they were so close to camp.

After two hours of creeping around camp, I discovered no more finds much to my disappointment.

As darkness fell I slowly stumbled into camp, and was astonished to find Podge and Ringo preparing dinner, (well Podge was cooking while Ringo was watching, maybe timing it).

I sat down next to the blazing fire as it crackled and lit up the surrounding area.

I fell asleep that night humming a song I was taught when I was young to keep calm and trying not to worry about the shadow that was lurking around camp.

So staring up at the sky and feeling hopeful knowing I will soon go home.

Day 27

As I strolled into the cave for my morning drink, I noticed the shadow that was plaguing my worries since yesterday, running from the cave opening and dashing again into the nearby brush.

I chased after it, but it was useless, the thing not only had a head start but seemed that it was super-fast and able to dodge me very well.

I then found myself shouting and cursing at the unknown thing, hoping that it would understand me. But also it would be frightened, so that it wouldn't come back to the mad screaming man that was cursing and slipping between English, Scottish and Australian accents.

As I walked back to camp, I found Ringo and Podge both waiting with perplex faces as if wondering what I was doing.

This made me wonder about the duo, they must have seen the thing for they were watching me as I went towards the cave.

All they did was watch me as I pondered the motives and reasons why they either didn't see it or were working with it for some unknown reason.

It was at this point I started to hope that they weren't part of anything sinister, but I knew I had to keep them both under my watchful eye.

So going back to the cave with the friendly duo in

tow, I went to the stream and had my morning drink as planned, I was shocked to find after I was done that whatever was stalking me was hiding in the shadows like the Imp from days ago waiting for the time to pounce.

I looked over at Podge but he was busy drinking though his "straw" tongue, I then looked over at Ringo but he stared back at me with what look like concern, I wasn't buying it, I knew they must be in on it and all three of them were planning on something very bad.

I stepped away slowly at first towards the entrance of the cave and once I saw light I burst out running with all of my might, passing not only bushes that stung and tree branches that slapped me as I dashed by, but I also saw creatures some familiar some new discoveries.

The rest of my day was ducking and hiding from anything that moved just in case, this annoyed me, I had cared for them and this is how they return the favour, plus what also pissed me off was the creatures I saw and couldn't study. Typical I had hours of boredom and there was animals I could have studied, where were they days ago. With my head banging and my arm throbbing, I settled in a nook between two rocks

Day 28

After a night of no sleep, on the move constantly dodging the noises and movement of possible killers, I've decided to write passage of my log when I can instead of waiting for ether last thing at night or first thing tomorrow morning.

While ducking and diving from anything that sounded like Ringo or Podge, I found the wreckage of my ship, the flames have gone out and the hull is collapsing at certain parts, in the air was the smell of burnt flesh decomposing on the ship I could see tiny sparks from some of the electronic stations still trying to function.

I didn't dare go inside but I settled nearby for the rescue whenever that is.

I have just started to hear noises from nearby and I have hidden, but it seemed that it was nothing; just wind streaming thought the destroyed ship wreckage.

My heart pounding, my energy has left me, pain grips my body constantly. Noises in my head hound me constantly. Slowly I drift off into darkness, I feel surrounded, I think they found me...

U.N.E. Verne +++ Rescue Log +++ Captain Lane Report

After war games in section 49386, we received a distress signal from the nearby Upsilon solar system.

Upon entering the system, we sent drone three to investigate the planet of the signal origin.

After a week drone three returned and the data was analysed, one life beacon was tracked so I and Security officer James Pickman and First Doctor Vera Langford boarded shuttle two and landed near the source of the signal.

After double checking the air was breathable we exited the shuttle and found the wreckage of the ship U.N.E. Space-hopper transport according to the black box that was recovered a few days later by a second recovery team along with twelve sets of charred remains.

We next check the Life Beacon tracker with no luck, so the three of us looked around for about a hundred yards and found one body that seem to have recently died and was missing a foot with two strange creatures yelping and guarding the body.

The body was that of delivery boy Mortimer Hanley according to the diary found nearby.

When anyone went near the body the creatures growled and snarled with such ferocity that I feared for the safety of my crew.

In the end I sat near the body and spoke softly to them, knowing for some reason that these creatures where not the killers of this poor boy, as Pickman suggested, but were protecting their friend. After about an hour I seemed to get through to the creatures and I decided to take not only the body when we was able but also the two creatures for something in my gut told me to. Pickman was not pleased.

The autopsy was done instantly while recovery team two started their mission, the autopsy concluded that Mr Shanley was suffering with a kind of blood poisoning and it must have been because of the wound upon his arm. Also it seemed that the victims' brain was infected with some kind of toxins at the same time and that this could of cause any kind of problems like delusions and irrational behaviour. I agreed that Mr Shanley was suffering from such symptoms going by the last days of his diary.

After two days of isolation, I decided to adopt the creatures known as Podge and Ringo for they seemed to be upset and missing their friend.

I also came to the conclusion that Mr Shanley's foot was removed by a creature he had called a Bite-weed. I conclude this by team two's find of a few of these creatures nearby and one of them was covered with dry blood that seemed to trail off towards the location of the body.

Full conclusion: all crewmen were killed either by the crash or by alien life forms.

Two alien creatures were recovered.

Final note: hopefully, the crew of the transport ship are at peace and sorry to Mr Shanley for not getting to him sooner and that hopefully he is happy and at peace that someone is now looking after Ringo and Podge.